Why do frogs sing?

Contents

Written by Jillian Powell

Illustrated by Rudolf Farkas

Collins

What's in this book?

Listen and say

nest

eggs

pond

leaves

frog

John and his mum were at the pond. John could hear lots of noise.

Chapter 1 Frog songs

There are 5,000 different frogs. They all have a different song.

Their songs mean, "This place is my home. Come and see!"

Frogs sing the loudest in the spring.

These spring peeper frogs are very small.
They sleep all winter and then in spring,
they wake up and sing.

spring peeper frog

Sometimes, it's difficult to know a frog song from other animal noises.

Is that noise a cow? No! It's this bull frog.

Is that noise a duck? No! It's this wood frog.

cow

bull frog

duck

wood frog

Chapter 2 Frog skin

Do you know frogs do not drink with their mouths? They drink with their skin.

Frogs' old skin falls off and the frog grows new skin. Some frogs get new skin every day, and some get new skin every week.

green and golden bell frog

Chapter 3 Frog babies

In the spring, you can see frogs' eggs in water. The eggs grow into tadpoles. The tadpoles grow legs. Then, they grow into baby frogs.

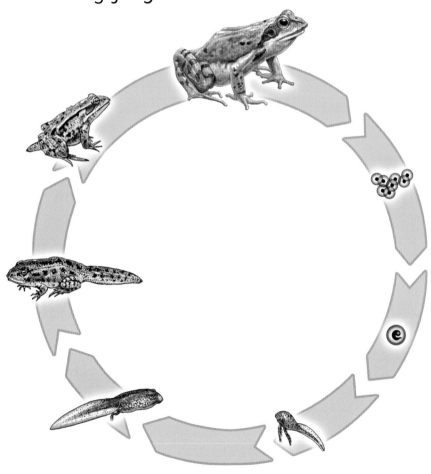

These poison dart frogs lay their eggs on the floor of the forest. The mother frogs watch their eggs. They want them to be safe.

eggs

The eggs grow into tadpoles. Then the tadpoles ride on their mother's back to get to the water.

poison dart frog

tadpole

These Suriname toads carry their eggs under their skin.

Suriname toad

These Darwin frog tadpoles grow in their father's mouths. The father Darwin frog carries its baby frogs to the water.

Darwin frog

These Asian tree frogs build a nest in a tree. They lay their eggs in the nest. The tadpoles drop into the water under the tree.

Asian tree frog

Chapter 4 Clever frogs

Frogs can do more than sing. These green tree frogs can climb trees. They jump from tree to tree to find their food. In the trees, they are safe from bigger animals.

green tree frog

These small Panamanian golden frogs
live next to rivers. The rivers make a lot
of noise. The frogs sometimes wave their
hands and feet, then their friends can
see them!

Panamanian golden frog

Frogs are many colours. The orange colour of these small mantella frogs tells animals in the forest, "Don't eat me. I can make you sick!"

mantella frog

These frogs can change the colours of their skin. Vietnamese mossy frogs are green. They hide in green plants.

Vietnamese mossy frog

The grey colour stops animals from seeing grey tree frogs.

grey tree frog

These North American wood frogs sleep in the cold winter. They hide in leaves. They wake up in the spring, and then they are ready to have babies. They start to sing again.

North American wood frog

Picture dictionary

Listen and repeat

hide

nest

pond

skin

tadpole

1 Look and say *"Yes"* or *"No"*

Frogs lay eggs.

Frogs grow into tadpoles.

Tadpoles grow legs.

Frogs have tails.

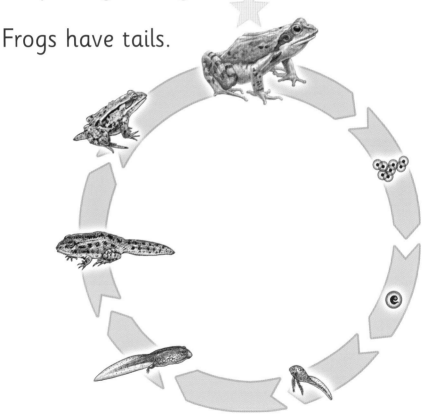

2 Listen and say

Collins

Published by Collins
An imprint of HarperCollins*Publishers*
Westerhill Road
Bishopbriggs
Glasgow
G64 2QT

HarperCollins*Publishers*
1st Floor, Watermarque Building
Ringsend Road
Dublin 4
Ireland

William Collins' dream of knowledge for all began with the publication of his first book in 1819.

A self-educated mill worker, he not only enriched millions of lives, but also founded a flourishing publishing house. Today, staying true to this spirit, Collins books are packed with inspiration, innovation and practical expertise. They place you at the centre of a world of possibility and give you exactly what you need to explore it.

© HarperCollins*Publishers* Limited 2020

10 9 8 7 6 5 4 3 2

ISBN 978-0-00-839696-1

Collins® and COBUILD® are registered trademarks of HarperCollins*Publishers* Limited

www.collins.co.uk/elt

British Library Cataloguing in Publication Data

A catalogue record for this publication is available from the British Library.

Author: Jillian Powell
Illustrator: Rudolf Farkas (Beehive)
Series editor: Rebecca Adlard
Commissioning editor: Fiona Undrill
Publishing manager: Lisa Todd
Product managers: Jennifer Hall and Caroline Green
In-house editor: Alma Puts Keren
Project manager: Emily Hooton
Editor: Matthew Hancock
Proofreaders: Natalie Murray and Michael Lamb
Cover designer: Kevin Robbins
Typesetter: 2Hoots Publishing Services Ltd
Audio produced by id audio, London
Reading guide author: Emma Wilkinson
Production controller: Rachel Weaver
Printed and bound by: GPS Group, Slovenia

MIX
Paper from responsible sources
FSC
www.fsc.org
FSC™ C007454

This book is produced from independently certified FSC™ paper to ensure responsible forest management.

For more information visit: **www.harpercollins.co.uk/green**

Download the audio for this book and a reading guide for parents and teachers at www.collins.co.uk/839696